# THE TECHNOLOGY OF
# ANCIENT GREECE

Charles W. Maynard

rosen
central™

The Rosen Publishing Group, Inc., New York

*This book is for Anastasia Katherine Lamar, the newest life in our family, and in memory of Dr. Royce Morris and in honor of Dr. Frederic Kellogg, my professors in Greek and in things Greek.*

Published in 2006 by The Rosen Publishing Group, Inc.
29 East 21st Street, New York, NY 10010

**Library of Congress Cataloging-in-Publication Data**

Maynard, Charles W. (Charles William), 1955–
The technology of ancient Greece/Charles W. Maynard.—1st ed.
    p. cm.—(The Technology of the ancient world)
Includes bibliographical references and index.
ISBN 1-4042-0555-1 (library binding)
1. Technology—Greece—History—To 146 B.C.—Juvenile literature. 2. Greece—Civilization—To 146 B.C.—Juvenile literature. I. Title. II. Series.
T16.M39 2005
609.38—dc22

2005013899

*Manufactured in the United States of America*

**On the cover:** Top: This terra-cotta figurine from about 520 to 480 BC was made in Thebes and shows a scribe writing on a tablet with a stylus. Bottom: Exekias painted this black-figure wine cup, called a *kylix*, in 540 BC. The scene depicts Dionysus, the Greek god of wine, in his ship (a trireme).

# CONTENTS

INTRODUCTION: ANCIENT GREECE,
BIRTHPLACE OF THE WESTERN WORLD  4

1 THE TECHNOLOGY OF AGRICULTURE AND TRADE  9

2 THE ART OF WRITING  17

3 THE BUILDING ARTS  23

4 THE STRATEGY OF WARFARE  32

5 THE TECHNOLOGY OF MEDICINE  39

TIMELINE  42

GLOSSARY  43

FOR MORE INFORMATION  44

FOR FURTHER READING  45

BIBLIOGRAPHY  46

INDEX  47

# INTRODUCTION

# ANCIENT GREECE, BIRTHPLACE OF THE WESTERN WORLD

The beginnings of present-day Western civilization are found in ancient Greece. In the ancient world, most civilizations began near some body of water—a sea, a river, or a lake. Ancient Greece was a loose collection of city-states, called poleis, spread over the Balkan and Peloponnesian peninsulas and numerous islands.

Ancient Greek history can be divided into four periods: the Bronze Age, the Dark Ages, the Classical Age, and the Hellenistic Age. The earliest days of the ancient Greeks are known as the Bronze Age, beginning around 2900 BC. The first Greeks settled the islands off the Greek coast in the Adriatic and Aegean seas. One of the first of these settlements, on the island of Crete, prospered between 2000 and 1450 BC. This group of settlers was called the Minoans, for the Cretan king Minos.

The Minoans flourished because of trade throughout the Greek islands, Egypt, Syria, and Asia Minor (part of present-day Turkey). This trade enriched the Minoans both culturally and financially. Much evidence of this great era in ancient Greece has been found in the ruins of palaces at Knossos, Mallia, Zakro, and Phaistos.

The Mycenaeans, who were from the town of Mycenae in Peloponnese, were a warlike people who invaded the Greek peninsula around 1600 BC. They traded with the Minoans and eventually began to

The Mycenaeans built the Lion Gate at the fortress of Mycenae around 1250 BC. The walls' huge blocks of stone were put together without cement and are called cyclopean, because it was thought that only the Cyclops, the one-eyed giant of Greek mythology, could have built them.

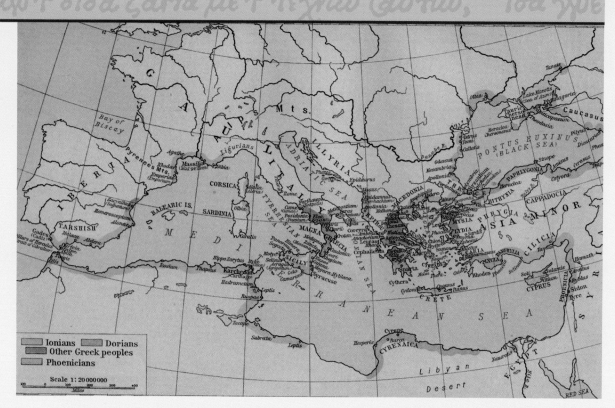

This map shows the extent of ancient Greek and Phoenician settlements in 550 BC. In ancient Greece, besides the city-state of Athens, there were the city-states of Corinth, Sparta, Thebes, and Thessalonica, and colonies located in Asia Minor and on islands in the Aegean Sea, southern Italy, and Sicily.

copy much of their culture, even adopting a form of their writing. The Mycenaean polis was often built around a high point (acropolis) with a stronghold for defense and temples for worship.

The Minoans, and later the Mycenaeans, traded throughout the Mediterranean Sea, so the Greek influence began to spread. However, around 1150 BC, the Mycenaean culture disintegrated, probably for a variety of related reasons. This began an era called the Dark Ages, during which the fortresses fell into decay and the small city-states collapsed.

After a little more than three centuries, the small city-states began to recover and prosper. This Classical Age, which began in the fifth century BC, was characterized by growth in the arts, philosophy, and technology. The word "technology" comes from the Greek words *techne*, meaning "art"

## WHAT TIME IS IT?

In the ancient world, sundials were used to tell time. These became better designed and more accurate in the sixth century BC. Ctesibius in the third century BC improved the clepsydra, or water clock, which had been used in Egypt since about 2000 BC. The clepsydra was used in Athens to time the length of orations and speeches in the court. It measured time by dripping water from one container into another. Hours were marked on the sides of either the container that received the water or the one from which it flowed. Some clepsydras floats were attached to gears that turned hands on a dial to indicate the time similar to clocks today.

*This clepsydra, or water clock, from the fifth century BC was discovered in the Athens agora (marketplace).*

or "craft," and *logos*, meaning "word" or "study." "Technology" has come to mean the "use of science and engineering to do practical things."

The Classical Age marked a high point in Greek architecture, the remnants of which can be seen in ruins throughout Greece and the Mediterranean coast from Spain to Turkey. The influence of the ancient Greeks lives on today in such buildings as the Lincoln Memorial and the Supreme Court Building in Washington, D.C.

Western literature, philosophy, medicine, and astronomy all have roots in the science and technology of ancient Greece. The word "alphabet" comes from the names for the first two letters of the Greek alphabet—alpha and beta. The Greek alphabet and the Roman alphabet, which is used to write English, are derived from the Phoenician alphabet.

Greek military prowess reached its height in the Hellenistic Age, with Alexander the Great (356–323 BC). Using the Greek phalanx and other military innovations, Alexander conquered the ancient world from Greece to India. He died a young man at the height of his powers in 323 BC. The Greeks continued to rule over this vast domain until they were conquered by Romans in 146 BC. The Romans copied many of the ideas, art, and technology of the Greeks. Despite defeat by the mighty Roman Empire, the Greeks continued to influence the world.

One legend of ancient Greece told of the inventor Daedalus. King Minos of Crete hired the renowned inventor to design and construct a labyrinth to contain the Minotaur. After the completion of the labyrinth, King Minos imprisoned Daedalus and his son, Icarus. The story goes that after the clever Daedalus fashioned wings of feathers and wax, he and his son flew to freedom. However, Icarus, in his youthful excitement, flew too high, too near the hot sun, and his wings melted. The young man plunged to his death in the sea far below, and his grief-stricken father flew to freedom in Sicily.

Like Daedalus, the Greeks of old were creative and inventive. Many of their innovations shaped and influenced our modern world. The ancient Greeks had eminent and creative thinkers who dreamed up many ways to work more easily and efficiently than any culture up to that time.

# THE TECHNOLOGY OF AGRICULTURE AND TRADE

The birth of botany, or the study of plants, is found in the works of the Greek philosopher Aristotle (384–322 BC) and his student Theophrastus (372–287 BC). Aristotle collected all types of plants. Later, in studying this collection, the young Theophrastus classified and named them. Consequently, Theophrastus is called the father of botany.

## People of the Land

In most of the ancient world, around the tenth century BC, a person or animal (such as an ox, cow, horse, or donkey) pulled a simple plow with a wooden or iron stake. First wooden, then bronze, and later iron, hoes chopped weeds and prepared the ground for the planting of seeds and the harvesting of crops. Bread and porridge formed a

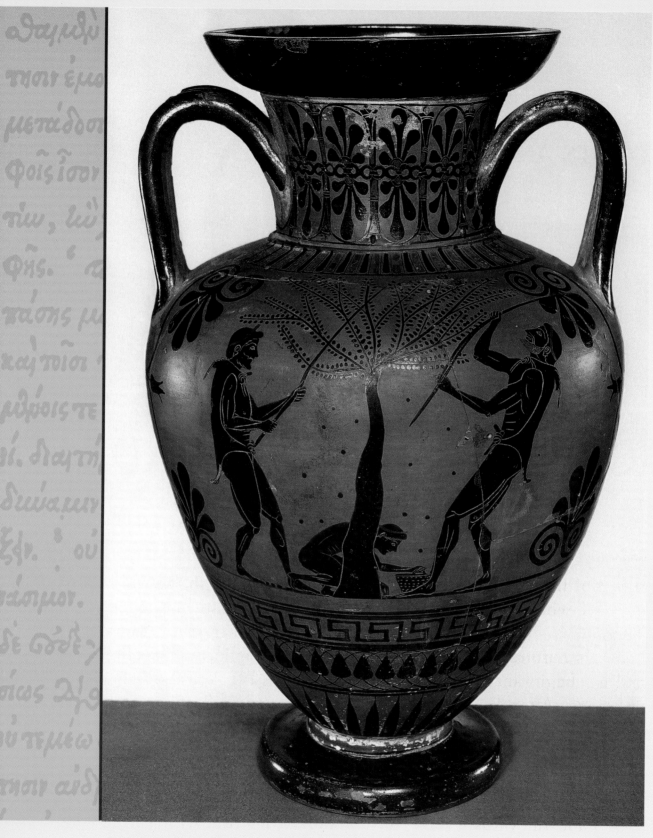

On this black-figure amphora from the late sixth century BC, men are depicted harvesting olives by swatting the tree with poles and then gathering the olives from the ground.

# OLIVES AND THEIR OIL

The Greeks had many uses for the olive tree. In midsummer, boys would climb the trees and knock down the ripe olives onto a cloth spread underneath the tree. Some olives were sold in the market to be eaten. Other olives were placed in a stone press. The olive oil press was made of two rounded stones that fit into another stone with a circle carved in it. Olive seeds were placed in the stone circle and the two rounded stones were rolled over the seeds, pressing out olive oil. When trees no longer produced much fruit, the hard wood was used to make household items such as boxes, tables, or chairs.

central part of the Greek diet, so the cultivation of wheat and barley was important.

The Greeks nurtured olive trees in large groves beginning in the first millennium BC. After harvest, stone presses squeezed the olives to get valuable oil that was used in cooking and lighting. Fruits such as figs, pears, apples, and pomegranates also grew in orchards. Grape vineyards were well-suited to the rocky and hilly soil of Greece. Wine was another important part of the Greek diet. Breakfast was

often a crust of bread dipped in wine and a few figs or other fruit.

Farmers raised animals as well as crops. Donkeys and oxen hauled heavy loads and pulled plows. Sheep and goats produced milk that was made into cheese. Small birds, chickens, goats, and sheep were sources of meat.

Technological innovations improved agriculture. Archimedes (287–212 BC) is credited with many inventions, including the compound pulley and the hydraulic screw for raising water. The Archimedes screw is a cylinder

A Greek farmer uses an ox-drawn plow in this terra-cotta sculpture from about 650 BC. Crops in ancient Greece included wheat, barley, pears, figs, olives, and grapes. The plows in ancient Greece were usually very simple devices made from tree branches.

with a wide-threaded screw inside that is turned by hand. The lower end of the cylinder is placed in water and as the screw is turned, the water slides along the thread of the screw and is lifted to a higher level. While he lived in Egypt, Archimedes invented the device to help with irrigation and drainage methods along the Nile River.

Improved agricultural methods resulted in greater production, which meant that the extra crops and food

had to be stored. Clay was shaped on a potter's wheel to form special types of ceramic pottery that were painted, glazed, and fired. (The potter's wheel had been invented most likely by the Mesopotamians around 3500 BC.) The amphora, a tall, two-handled vessel, was used to store wine, honey, or oil. A shipwreck of a merchant ship from the fourth century BC, found off the coast of Cyprus in the late 1960s, contained a cargo of more than 400

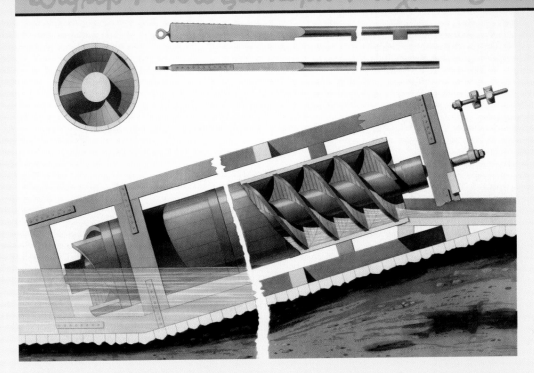

Archimedes has been credited as the inventor of a screw device that pumped water from rivers to irrigate land. This version of his screw has a thread of spiral-shaped metal on a central post with a handle attached to the top. This was placed inside a cylinder, and the end of the mechanism was positioned in water. When the handle was turned, water would get trapped in the spirals of the tube, and would gradually rise to the top.

amphorae and a large shipment of almonds that was still intact.

Over time, the potters decorated their creations with intricate pictures of the life and legends of ancient Greece. Around 720 BC to 500 BC, a black-figure technique of decoration was popular. Black silhouetted figures were painted on a reddish clay background. A bone or metal tool was used to cut the fine details on the figures.

Just after 500 BC, potters began to use a red-figure technique, which meant that the figures were left in the red clay and the background was painted with a clay solution that turned black during firing.

## A Seafaring People

In ancient Greece, most city-states and settlements were not far from the sound of waves and the salty smell of the sea. Those farthest inland were

**A fisher holds his catch of the day. This wall painting was found in AD 1967, in a house that had been buried during a volcanic eruption on the Greek island of Thira in the 1500s BC. The artistic style of the painting shows Cretan and Minoan influences, two groups that frequently traded with the Thirans.**

located only about forty miles (sixty kilometers) from the sea. The Greeks depended heavily upon fishing as a food source. Seafood, such as mackerel, octopus, and squid, was always on the table. Small boats with oars and sails were used to fish the blue waters of the Aegean Sea.

The small boats could not venture far from the shore because navigation required the boat to be in sight of land. However, as boats and ships improved and larger sailing vessels were made, the astrolabe and star charts were developed to aid in navigation. The astrolabe measured the position of stars and planets. It was a circle or semicircle marked off in degrees. An arm fixed at the center of the circle was used to point at a particular star. The altitude of the star from the horizon could then be determined. Greek ships plied the Mediterranean Sea far from their own Aegean waters. These great ships took large shipments of oil, wine, tapestries, and pottery to distant ports.

## Trade and Commerce

The soil in Greece is rocky and the terrain is hilly, making farming difficult. Wet winters and dry growing seasons only added to the problems of producing enough food to sustain the population. The Greeks had to rely on trade to survive. Olives, olive oil, wine, and pottery were traded for grain.

To assist in the transfer of goods, the Greeks adopted the use of coins from Lydia in Asia Minor. The first coins, minted in the seventh century BC, were irregular in shape and were made of a mixture of gold and silver called electrum. By 575 BC, Athens minted its own coins. Before this time the Athenians used iron and long nails as money.

Early coins had an image stamped on only one side. These images featured a variety of animals—eagles, horses, owls, and goats. Sometimes the animal had a special meaning to the people of one city. For instance, Athenians revered the owl, so many of their coins had an owl on them. Occasionally, mythical creatures, such as Pegasus or the Minotaur, were used. The value of each coin was determined by its own weight. The drachma was a silver coin, minted in Athens, that became common throughout the region. This unique innovation of coinage allowed traders to use coins instead of other goods as they would in a barter system of trade.

In trade and commerce, Athens and Corinth began to dominate other city-states. Both had good ports and produced many trade goods. Corinth was ideally located on one side of a narrow isthmus. Trade goods were often hauled across the isthmus to avoid the long trip around the Peloponnesian peninsula. Ships were rolled on logs and large-wheeled

**An owl representing the city-state of Athens is stamped on this tetradrachm, a silver coin from around 500 BC. To create the images on coins, the ancient Greeks used stamps, which were prepared from two dies (one for each side). A hammer and punch were used to strike the metal and produce the designs.**

vehicles over land across the isthmus. Corinth became rich as a port city with international connections.

Due to the rich trade and good ships of the Greeks, their influence and power spread throughout the Mediterranean. In the seventh and sixth centuries BC, the Greeks established colonies as far away as present-day Spain, Tunisia, and Egypt. With these colonies spread the Greek language, architecture, and culture.

# THE ART
# OF WRITING

In prehistoric times, people drew pictures on cave walls to tell stories. The earliest forms of writing were pictographs, which were symbols used to represent objects. The symbol for a star was simply a small picture of a star. A picture of a bull represented that animal. The ancient Egyptian system of pictographs, with its hundreds of symbols, was called hieroglyphics. (Present-day Chinese is a pictographic form of writing with thousands of symbols.) Pictograph systems of writing gradually changed to systems that used symbols to represent sounds. The sound was usually the initial sound of a word portrayed by a pictograph. For instance, in early Hebrew, a picture of a house, *beth*, came to stand for the letter *b*.

The first type of writing in Greece is called Linear A and was used by the Minoans in the second millennium BC. Sometime later,

This tablet with Linear A script *(top)*, from about 1500 to 1400 BC, is from the palace at Knossos in Crete. The Minoans wrote this syllabic script from left to right. This stone tablet *(bottom)*, from the palace of Nestor at Pylos, is an example of Linear B writing of the second millennium BC.

around 1400 BC, Mycenaean priests developed a type of writing called Linear B that used syllable groups to form words. They took symbols from Linear A and added others to form their own writing. This type of writing was most often used for record keeping, especially for the palace goods.

When the Mycenaean civilization collapsed, its style of writing disappeared with it. At about the same time, however, the Phoenicians developed an alphabet using symbols to represent sounds. Later, when the Greeks traded with the Phoenicians in the eighth century BC, they based their alphabet on the Phoenician one. The Phoenicians had an alphabet with only consonants. The Greeks added symbols for vowels and came up with twenty-four characters.

# THE GREEK ALPHABET

| | | | | | | | | |
|---|---|---|---|---|---|---|---|---|
| A | α | alpha | a | | M | μ | mu | m |
| B | β | beta | b | | N | ν | nu | n |
| Γ | γ | gamma | g | | Ξ | ξ | xi | x, ks |
| Δ | δ | delta | d | | O | o | omicron | o |
| E | ε | epsilon | e | | Π | π | pi | p |
| Z | ζ | zeta | z | | P | ρ | rho | r |
| H | η | eta | long e, sometimes long a | | Σ | σ ς | sigma | s |
| | | | | | T | τ | tau | t |
| Θ | θ | theta | th | | Y | υ | upsilon | u |
| I | ι | iota | i | | Φ | φ | phi | ph |
| K | κ | kappa | c, k | | X | χ | chi | ch |
| Λ | λ | lambda | l | | Ψ | ψ | psi | ps |
| | | | | | Ω | ω | omega | long o |

Earliest Greek was written from right to left, as was Phoenician. Eventually, the first line was written from left to right while the second line was written from right to left and the third from left to right, and so on, like an ox plowing a field. By about the sixth century BC, Greek was written entirely from left to right.

Rulers and generals used writing to govern large areas and move huge armies. Reports were written, and laws were recorded and reproduced. Commands were clearer and more easily carried to far-flung outposts than verbal orders that could be forgotten or misinterpreted. Greek became an international language throughout the Mediterranean basin for trade and governance.

## Uses of Writing

The earliest method of writing by the Minoans and the Mycenaeans used a stylus on clay tablets. Examples of Linear A and Linear B on clay were discovered by archaeologists after AD 1900. As the Greek alphabet

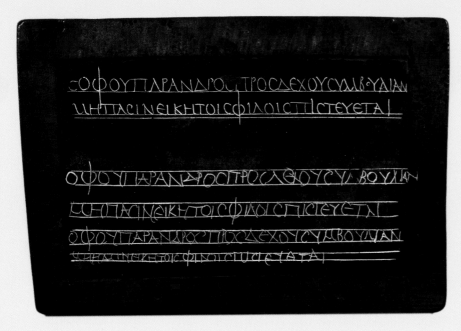

was developed, other methods of writing became widely used. School-boys and merchants used a wooden or bone stylus to mark wax tablets. These tablets could be smoothed over and reused.

As the Greek alphabet was developed, reading and writing became more common. In addition to lists and documents for trade, people began writing for entertainment. Homer (eighth century BC) is generally recognized as the author of two epic poems, *The Iliad* and *The Odyssey. The Iliad* tells of the final stages of the Trojan War between Greek city-states and Troy, while *The Odyssey* describes the ten-year return journey

of Odysseus at the close of the Trojan War.

By the sixth century BC, the Greeks were writing plays. At first these were dramas of historic events and legends, such as the Trojan War, but comedies about the ways of life were added later. The Greeks constructed large amphitheaters that could hold 14,000 to 20,000 people for the performance of these plays. Cities conducted annual contests to determine the prize plays for the year.

Three of the early dramatists were Aeschylus (circa 525–456 BC), Sophocles (circa 496–406 BC), and Euripides (circa 480–406 BC). These great writers wrote hundreds of plays in

In ancient Greece, schoolchildren used wax writing tablets, similar to the one pictured at the far left, to practice penmanship. This wax tablet from the second century BC contains two lines at the top that were written as models. Students then copied these lines below, between ruled lines. This red-figure drinking cup *(above)* shows a school scene from the fifth century BC, depicting a student using a writing tablet and stylus.

the fifth century BC, when Greek drama flourished, but only thirty-one of these plays survived into modern times. Scholars and schoolchildren continue to study and perform them today.

Writing was also important in recording the events of the past. Herodotus (circa 484–425 BC) is known as the father of history because he wrote the customs, legends, histories, and traditions of the ancient world. He is particularly remembered for his histories of the wars between Greece and Persia. It is possible that Herodotus's work may be the first example of prose writing, because poems and plays were written in verse. The word "history" comes from a Greek word, *historia*, meaning "inquiry."

Ink made of lampblack, glue, and water and pens of sharpened reeds were first used on papyrus, a paper made of reeds mashed together and smoothed with pumice stones. Rolls of papyrus about twenty to thirty feet (six to nine meters) long were most common for compiling written materials in the Hellenistic and Roman periods. These were large and sometimes difficult to use. If the roll had to be used often, the ends of it wore out. Even though papyrus was easily and cheaply made, and provided a good writing surface, it was brittle in damp climates and fell apart in less than 100 years.

## The First Books

The first "books" were probably small ringed notebooks used for accounting or schoolwork. Two joined, wax-covered, wooden tablets, called a diptych, were written on with a stylus. Papyrus sheets could be inserted between the tablets. Later, around 200 BC, parchment was developed. Parchment was made from the untanned skins of sheep, calves, or goats. It was a much more durable writing surface than papyrus, and it gradually replaced the use of papyrus. Sheets of parchment were stacked and bound together to form a codex, which was another step toward making present-day books. Some of the earliest parchment codices in existence today are portions of the Bible dating from the fourth and fifth centuries AD.

The Greek world was famous for its enormous library at the Greek city of Alexandria in Egypt. It is said that this library contained more than 500,000 volumes, making it the largest collection of scrolls, codices, and books in the ancient world. This library was destroyed over many centuries, and most of the works held there were lost. Another famous library was at Pergamum in modern-day Turkey.

Today, the Greek alphabet is still in use. The Cyrillic alphabet, used to write Russian, is based on the Greek alphabet. Many mathematical symbols are Greek letters. The best known of these is $\pi$ (pronounced "pi"), which is used to represent the ratio of the circumference of a circle to its diameter.

Scholars continue to study the ancient Greek texts of plays, poems, and the Bible to increase their understanding of the culture and thinking of the early Greeks.

# THE BUILDING ARTS

The Greeks are known for their columned temples, where they worshipped and made sacrifices to their gods. The Temple of Hera at Olympia, the Temple of Ceres at Paestum, and the Sanctuary of Apollo at Delphi are three famous examples. The remains of the original Parthenon built in the fifth century BC still stand on the Acropolis in Athens.

## Early Construction of the Minoans and Mycenaeans

The Minoans built temples and palaces on Crete during the Bronze Age. Remains of these buildings have been unearthed by archaeologists since the late AD 1800s. These Minoan buildings reveal great ability and skill in construction. The palace at Knossos on Crete was constructed around 1900 BC and is an example of this

Among the ruins at the palace at Knossos, Crete, is the grand staircase, with columns that taper toward the bases. King Minos reportedly had the architect Daedalus build the palace, which included a multistoried complex with wall paintings, a central courtyard, a theater, royal chambers, and a labyrinth, which housed the mythological Minotaur.

architecture. This enormous palace encompassed a whole settlement, which had hundreds of rooms grouped around a central courtyard and could house thousands of people. The lack of defensive walls shows that the Minoans did not fear any enemies.

In Mycenae, tombs, palaces, and city walls were built of large stones. The Lion Gate at Mycenae can still be viewed as an example of this early construction. The fact that it still exists testifies to the skilled crafting of huge stones atop a slightly curved lintel that spreads the weight to the posts on each side. Lions were carved in the triangular stones over the lintel.

Tools were simple and crude at first. Although no one can be certain, Theodorus of Samos in the sixth century BC is credited with inventing and developing the water level, the lock and key, the carpenter's square, and the turning lathe. He is also known as a sculptor who developed ore smelting and the casting of bronze statues. These were all important milestones in the development of building technology.

## Houses

Houses were simple structures in ancient Greece. The poorer people lived in small, one-room houses. The wealthier lived in larger houses that wrapped around a small interior court-yard often containing an altar to a family god. Most houses were built of sun-dried bricks covered with plaster. Wood was scarce, so only the doors and windows were made of it. The roofs were built of clay tiles shaped to drain rainwater. Artisans put clay into wooden forms made into the desired shape. These tiles were then fired to make the roof tiles. Archaeologists sometimes discover small hearths that were used as kitchens. People brought baking dishes to a community oven.

Some houses had elaborate artwork of colored pebbles arranged into mosaics depicting scenes of Greek history or mythology. Frescoes, or paintings made on wet plaster walls, decorated houses and public buildings with images of animals, people, or gods. The largest houses had an *andron*, or dining room, in which men entertained their male friends while the family ate in a separate room. A

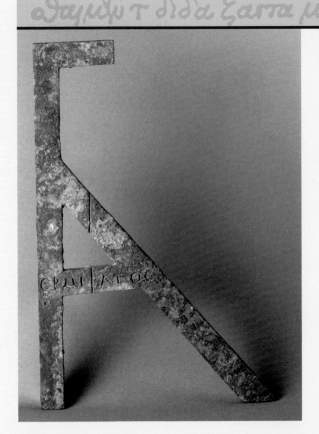

**Theodorus of Samos (sixth century BC) is credited with inventing the carpenter's square, similar to the bronze one pictured here, as well as the water level, the lock and key, and the turning lathe. The carpenter's square was a valuable tool in the construction of temples.**

This terra-cotta model of a Minoan house is from Archanes, Crete, and was made around 1600 BC. It shows a two-storied house, with an inner courtyard on the first floor and a room with an attached porch on the second floor. Common elements in Classical Greek architecture, such as the porch, columns, and inner courtyard, can be seen in this small Minoan model.

bathroom in the house included a large bathing pool but no toilet, which was usually in a small building away from the house. Some towns had a community bathroom with lots of toilets for everyone.

## Temples

Temples were viewed as houses for the gods. Like houses, the earliest temples were simple one-room buildings with flat roofs supported by tree trunks. These small temples housed the statue of a god or goddess and protected the sacrifices or offerings left by people.

The Greeks used simple post and lintel construction for their rectangular temples. When trees became more scarce by the fifth century BC, limestone and marble were shaped into

# COLUMN STYLES

The Greeks used three different styles of columns in the construction of temples and other buildings. The first and most popular is the Doric style that has a fluted (having vertical grooves) column of stone with a simple capital (top). The Ionic style came later and had more pronounced flutes on the columns with scroll-like decorations on the capitals. The scrolls were probably based on whelk shells and other natural spiral shapes. Later still, the Corinthian designs displayed elaborate acanthus leaf and scroll designs on the capitals. This last style was very popular with the Roman conquerors of Greece in the second century BC.

*Doric capital*

*Ionic capital*

*Corinthian capital*

blocks and columns. Arches and vaults were in use in other parts of the world, but the Greeks seemed to prefer the "wood" style of architecture with the post and lintel design.

Ten-ton (9.07-metric-ton) blocks of stone were quarried and shaped before being transported to the building site by cart and oxen. The marble for the Parthenon in Athens came from a quarry 10 miles (16 km) from Athens. Wooden wedges were hammered down into the marble. When water was poured on the wedges, the wood swelled and cracked the marble. Craftsmen chiseled off

The Roman architect and engineer Vitruvius (first century BC) described the cranes that were used by the ancient Greeks in building temples. The bottom illustration shows engineers positioning marble blocks to make columns. The top illustration depicts the methods for hoisting and moving blocks of stone, either by using rope or tongs.

corners to form the blocks into cylindrical sections called drums with four lugs projecting from the sides. These lugs made it possible for the sections to be lifted with ropes and pulleys.

Upon their arrival at the building site, sections were further fashioned into the needed design and shape.

These sections were lifted into place by workmen on scaffolds. Man-powered cranes equipped with pulleys and winches were used to lift the stones into place. When the section was in place and secured, the protruding lugs were chiseled off.

Craftsmen and sculptors fashioned many statues and ornaments to beautify

# THE EUPALINOS TUNNEL

In 530 BC, construction of a tunnel under Mount Kastro on Samos began. The engineer Eupalinos is credited with building this 3,400-foot (1036 m) tunnel. This project used crews that started on each side of the mountain and dug toward each other. The giant effort took ten years to complete. When the two sides met, they were only 23.6 inches (60 centimeters) off! It is estimated that more than 247,200 cubic feet (7,000 cubic meters) of rock were removed from under the mountain. The tunnel was part of a larger aqueduct project designed to bring water to Samos.

temples. The band around the eaves of the temple roof, the frieze, often included statues of figures from Greek history. The pediment, the triangular section under the roof line on each end of the building, had larger-than-life–sized statues that depicted a scene from Greek mythology or history. Statues and altars were masterfully carved works of art to honor the gods.

## The Parthenon

According to most scholars, the Parthenon is the finest example of temple construction, with eight columns on the front and back, and seventeen on the sides. It was begun on the Acropolis of Athens in 447 BC. Greek architects Ictinus and Callicrates designed the Parthenon to embody the Greek ideals of beauty, harmony, and proportion. Built of marble, the Parthenon measured 101 feet (30.8 m) wide by 228 feet (69.5 m) long. The great sculptor Phidias fashioned the statue of Athena, for whom the temple was built, and also supervised the many other carvers who worked on the temple. It is estimated that it took more than 10 million skilled workdays to complete the Parthenon in 432 BC.

Phidias's 40-foot (12 m) statue of Athena was said to have been covered

An aerial view of the Acropolis in Athens shows the upper fortified portion of the city where the Parthenon *(top right)*, the Erectheum *(left)*, and the Temple of Athena Nike *(foreground right)* are located. The construction of the Parthenon and its sculpture are considered the high point of technology in Classical Greek architecture.

with more than 2,500 pounds (1,136 kilograms) of gold. Her outstretched arms, welcoming Athenians to worship her, were sculpted in ivory. Many other sculptures portraying scenes from Athena's birth and life adorned the pediments of the temples. Other sculptures and decorations were added to the frieze to further embellish this most famous example of classical structures. Phidias also made a similar statue, Zeus, in Olympia, and it became known as one of the Seven Wonders of the Ancient World.

## Public Buildings

In Athens, as well as in other city-states, temples and various public buildings were constructed on the acropolis. These high places were probably first used as fortresses to defend the city from enemies. Builders flattened these hills and built other structures on them. A city's importance and wealth were displayed in its public buildings.

Sculptors made statues of marble and of bronze. Their superior technical and artistic skills caused the stone and bronze figures to appear almost lifelike. The Romans copied the style of many Greek statues because of the Greeks' artistry. Some statues even had mechanical parts that could move.

In addition to temples and public buildings, the Greeks constructed amphitheaters into hillsides. These amphitheaters, which could hold up to 20,000 people, were built for the performance of plays that were presented at annual festivals to Dionysus, the god of wine. Because there was no sound equipment, the builders designed the amphitheaters so that everyone could hear the words of the actors and chorus no matter where they were sitting.

Stadiums and hippodromes were built for spectators to watch sporting events, such as foot and chariot races, boxing matches, discus throwing, and javelin throwing. The most famous of these stadiums is in Olympia, where the first Olympics were held to honor Zeus, the king of the gods, in 776 BC.

# THE STRATEGY OF WARFARE

The Mycenaeans were warlike and aggressive, and controlled mainland Greece from about 1600 to 1200 BC. From them come the defining epics of Greece—*The Iliad* and *The Odyssey*—accounts of the Trojan War and the return to Greece written in the eighth century BC. The legendary Helen, wife of Menelaus, the king of Sparta, was stolen by Paris of Troy. The Mycenaeans, led by King Agamemnon, Menelaus's brother, sailed to Troy to avenge this wrong and rescue Helen. According to the myth, after a ten-year struggle and siege, the Mycenaeans built a large wooden horse in which they hid a few soldiers. When the rest of the troops left, the Trojans brought the horse inside the city walls thinking it was a gift. At nightfall, the hidden Mycenaeans climbed out to open the city gates for their army, and Troy was attacked.

This relief from the fourth century BC shows a charioteer and a warrior riding a quadriga. A quadriga is a chariot that is drawn by four horses abreast. Most Greek chariots were constructed to be drawn by two horses. The basket of the chariot rested on the axle, and there were no seats so the driver and passenger had to stand.

## Land Warfare

The story of the Trojan horse is illustrative of the Greeks' innovation in warfare. In ancient Egypt and Mesopotamia, the chariot and cavalry were used to win battles. However, in the fourth century BC, the Greeks developed a formation of foot soldiers called the phalanx. A phalanx was a rectangular arrangement of hoplites (foot soldiers) eight rows deep. Each man was armed with a short 1.5- to 2-foot (0.46 to 0.60 m) double-edged sword, a round shield, and a 15-foot (4.6 m) spear. These spears were long enough that those of the men in the fifth rank would reach past those in the first rank. Thus, an approaching enemy would face a wall of armored men bristling with spears. Before advancing, the hoplites would sing a battle hymn, then march forward to the sound of drums and music played by young boys.

A hoplite's body armor consisted of a helmet, a cuirass, and greaves, all made of bronze. The cuirass protected the upper body with breast- and backplates that were joined on the sides with leather. The lower legs were sheathed in bronze leggings called greaves, which were similar to shin guards. This armor could weigh up to 70 pounds (32 kg). Because the soldiers were required to pay for their own equipment and armor, only wealthy men could be hoplites.

## Persian Wars

Sometimes one city-state would attack another. These battles were usually quick and deadly. However, when the Persians invaded Greece in 490 BC, the city-states united to oppose them. Persian emperors Darius and Xerxes led enormous armies against the outnumbered Greeks. Between 490 and

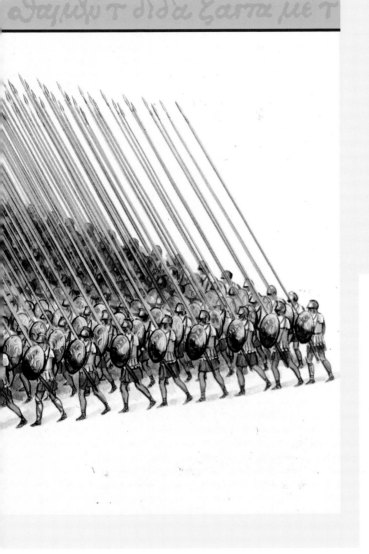

This modern watercolor shows the phalanx formation used by Macedonians. Here, 256 foot soldiers stand in rows of sixteen by sixteen. Each hoplite soldier carried a double-edged sword, a round shield, and a long spear.

## Sparta

Sparta developed a strong army after being defeated by an enemy. All boys began training for the military when they were seven years old. The training was made difficult to harden them to the rigors of battle. All men served in the army as adults. Spartan soldiers proudly wore scarlet military cloaks. Athens and Sparta were rival city-states that occasionally united to fight common enemies, such as the Persians. The war between the two cities and their allies was called the Peloponnesian War, and finally ended with the defeat of Athens by Sparta in 404 BC.

## Sea Warfare

Another legendary battle with the Persians was fought at sea. The Greeks had large warships called triremes that were fast and well armed. A trireme

479 BC, in a series of battles on land and sea, the Greeks defeated the Persians, who finally retreated to their own country. One famous battle took place in September 490 BC at Marathon, where the Persians lost 6,400 soldiers to the Athenians' 192. It was in the aftermath of this battle that a messenger ran the 24 miles (38.6 km) from Marathon to Athens to tell the Athenians about the defeat of the Persians so the city would not surrender to the Persian navy.

# INVENTOR SAVES SYRACUSE!

"Inventor Saves Syracuse!" could have been the headline in 213 BC, when the Romans attacked the Greek colony of Syracuse on Sicily. Although Archimedes was known for his many inventions and discoveries and was not a warrior, it is said that he brought several of his mechanical devices to the aid of his city. Among the machines he is thought to have invented is the catapult, a device for throwing large stones or flaming materials great distances. Legend says that he devised a system of mirrors that focused the sun's light on the Roman ships and set them afire. Archimedes saved the day, and the Romans retreated. Later, however, the Romans did take the city.

*In this wall painting, a Greek uses a mirror and the sun's rays to set Roman ships on fire in a battle between Romans and Syracuse in 213 BC. Archimedes was said by some people to have developed the use of mirrors as a weapon to reflect the sun's rays and cause ships to burn.*

**Because the sea was a significant part of their lives, the Greeks excelled in shipbuilding. The trireme, such as the one shown in this relief from Classical Greece, was a fast battleship, which required 170 oarsmen to row it. It also had a sturdy battering ram on the bow that was used for sinking enemy ships.**

used 170 men who sat on three levels to row it. The bow of these ships was pointed so that the ship could ram other ships. Fifty more soldiers and commanders manned the uppermost deck and could attack a ship once it was rammed. The triremes were about 128 feet (39 m) long and 15 feet (4.6 m) wide. The triremes were fitted with square-rigged sails, which were not used in battle because the direction of the wind was not dependable. The sails were used to move the ships from place to place while the oarsmen rowed the large ships to gain ramming speed. It is said that the trireme was able to reach speeds of 7 knots or 8 miles per hour (13 km/h) and as high as 9 knots or 10.4 miles per hour (16.7 km/h) with oars.

## Siege Warfare

Not all battles were fought in the open. In some battles, an army

# ALEXANDER THE GREAT

The greatest Greek soldier was Alexander of Macedon. As a boy, Alexander was tutored by the philosopher Aristotle. The son of King Philip II, Alexander (356–323 BC) became king at the age of twenty, when his father was murdered. Alexander took the 35,000-man army his father had gathered and trained, and invaded Greece's longtime enemy, Persia. Alexander defeated the Persian army at the Battle of Issus in 333 BC. He continued his conquests in Egypt, Babylon, and India. However, when his army refused to march any farther upon reaching northwest India in 326 BC, he began his return. At that time, his empire was the largest of the ancient empires. Alexander died of a fever in 323 BC in Babylon at the age of thirty-two. Alexander's influence and legacy far outlasted his short life.

attacked a walled city. Although smaller versions of the catapult were used on the battlefield to shoot large arrows, spears, or small stones, larger ones threw boulders and burning material over high city walls.

Siege towers with bridges were built to scale the defensive walls of a city. Sometimes the base of the tower had a battering ram. Battering rams knocked holes in the city's wall or broke down its heavy gates. The battering ram also could be covered so that the attackers would be protected from the arrows of the city's defenders.

Greek innovation in warfare reached its height with Alexander the Great. The Greeks conquered much of the known world and spread their language, literature, art, and culture throughout those areas.

# THE TECHNOLOGY OF MEDICINE

The ancient world believed that illness was a result of fate or a punishment from the gods. In early Greece, when a person became ill, he or she was taken to the Temple of Asclepius, the god of medicine and healing. People believed that if they prayed to Asclepius and spent the night in the temple, they would dream of a cure. Priests at the temples assisted in carrying out the cures of which people dreamed.

The sick bathed carefully before entering the temple, and gave an offering of honey cakes on the altar. The patient would then lie down on a mat in silence and go to sleep in hopes of receiving a cure in a dream. When a person was cured, he or she would return to the temple with a terra-cotta or plaster model of the part of the body that was healed as an offering of thanks to Asclepius.

Asclepius was the Greek god of medicine. He is depicted caring for a bedridden patient in this marble relief from the fifth century BC. Asclepius is often shown carrying his attribute, a staff that is entwined with a snake. The snake is a symbol for rebirth because it sheds its old skin.

In *The Iliad*, Homer described nearly 150 wounds in great detail, showing that even in the eighth century BC, much was known about the body. Homer mentioned surgery as one way to heal wounds, in addition to herbal medicines. This is one of the earliest known writings about surgery as a part of medicine.

Hippocrates (460–377 BC), from the island of Kos, taught that illnesses were not a punishment by the gods.

Instead, he carefully watched and studied people who were ill to understand sickness in a scientific way. He examined patients, and then prescribed herbal medicines, rest, special diets, and exercise. He believed healers should live with honor and uprightness. Hippocrates suggested a philosophy of life that included health and wholeness. Physicians today still take the Hippocratic oath, promising to follow a special code of ethics.

# THE HIPPOCRATIC OATH

The Hippocratic oath was developed by Hippocrates of Kos and his followers as a code of ethics for those in the healing arts. It is still used by doctors today.

You do solemnly swear, each by whatever he or she holds most sacred; that you will be loyal to the Profession of Medicine and just and generous to its members; that you will lead your lives and practice your art in uprightness and honor . . . that you will exercise your art solely for the cure of your patients, and will give no drug, perform no operation, for a criminal purpose, even if solicited, far less suggest it; that whatsoever you shall see or hear of the lives of men or women which is not fitting to be spoken, you will keep inviolably secret. These things do you swear . . . And now, if you will be true to this, your oath, may prosperity and good repute be ever yours; the opposite, if you shall prove yourselves forsworn.

Because of his work and writings, Hippocrates is known as the father of modern medicine. The idea of preventive medicine is in the *Hippocratic Collection*, which proposes that a person's lifestyle influences his or her health and recovery.

Greek medicine continued to progress with the work of Herophilus (third century BC), who performed the first public dissection to understand clearly what makes up the body or anatomy. He proposed that the brain was the center of the nervous system. Erasistratus (mid–third century BC) studied the circulation system and attempted to understand the veins, arteries, and heart.

# TIMELINE

| | |
|---|---|
| 2900 BC | Bronze Age begins. |
| 2000 BC | Minoan culture develops on Crete. |
| 1700 BC | Mycenaean culture develops on the Greek peninsula. |
| 1250 BC | Troy is destroyed by Mycenaeans. |
| 800 BC | The alphabet is developed. The Greeks add vowels to Phoenician consonants. |
| 800–701 BC | *The Iliad* by Homer refers to highly developed surgery on the battlefield. |
| 776 BC | The Olympic Games begin. |
| 650 BC | The trireme is developed. |
| 500 BC | The Classical Age begins. Eupalinos builds a tunnel. |
| 479–431 BC | The golden years of Athens. The Parthenon is built. |
| 460 BC | Hippocrates of Kos is born. |
| 400 BC | An arrow-shooting catapult is developed at Syracuse. |
| 336 BC | The Hellenistic Age begins. |
| 336–323 BC | Alexander the Great rules Greece. |
| 287–212 BC | Archimedes lives. |
| 170 BC | Parchment is invented in Pergamon. |
| 146 BC | Rome conquers Greece. |

# GLOSSARY

**acropolis** "High city" in Greek. A central hill in a Greek city-state that was first used as a fortress and later for temples.

**amphora** Large, two-handled pottery jars used for storing wine and olive oil.

**andron** Room in which the master of a house entertained male guests.

**astrolabe** An instrument used for measuring the positions of the sun and stars.

**Bronze Age** Historical period from 3000 to 1100 BC.

**city-state** A small state that developed around a city or island in ancient Greece.

**Classical Age** Historical period from 500 to 336 BC.

**codex** An early book made of parchment or papyrus.

**democracy** A system of government in which all citizens have a vote.

**drachma** Silver coin issued by the city of Athens.

**epic poem** A long story poem about heroic adventures and great battles.

**fresco** Painting technique in which paint is applied to wet plaster.

**frieze** Sculptures in a band around the eaves of a temple.

**Hellenistic Age** Historical period from 336 to 147 BC.

**isthmus** A narrow piece of land connecting two larger land areas.

**labyrinth** A maze.

**lathe** A machine that rotates a piece of wood or metal that is shaped by a cutting tool.

**lintel** The horizontal piece of wood or stone over a door or window.

**Minoan** Relating to a civilization based in Crete from 2000 to 1450 BC, named for King Minos.

**Minotaur** A legendary creature that was half man, half bull and lived in the labyrinth of King Minos.

**Mycenaean** Relating to a civilization based on the Peloponnesian peninsula from 1700 to 1200 BC.

**pediment** The triangular end of a roof that is filled with sculptures.

**phalanx** A battle formation of foot soldiers, or hoplites, in which the soldiers march side by side in a block.

**polis** A Greek city-state. The plural of "polis" is "poleis."

**trireme** A Greek warship with three banks of oars.

# FOR MORE INFORMATION

The Archaeological Institute of America
Boston University
656 Beacon Street, Fourth Floor
Boston, MA 02215
(617) 353-9361
Web site: http://www.archaeological.org

*Dig! The Archaeology Magazine for Kids*
30 Grove Street, Suite C
Peterborough, NH 03458
(800) 821-0115
Web site: http://www.digonsite.com

Metropolitan Museum of Art
1000 Fifth Avenue
New York, NY 10028
Web site: http://www.metmuseum.org

## In Canada

Ontario Archaeological Society
1444 Queen Street, E
Toronto, ON M4L 1E1
(416) 406-5959
Web site: http://www.
  ontarioarchaeology.on.ca

Royal Ontario Museum
100 Queen's Park
Toronto, ON M5S 2C6
(416) 586-5549
Web site: http://www.rom.on.ca

Smithsonian Institution Information
P.O. Box 37012
SI Building, Room 153, MRC010
Washington, DC 20013
(202) 633-2000
Web site: http://www.si.edu

## Web Sites

Due to the changing nature of Internet links, the Rosen Publishing Group, Inc., has developed an online list of Web sites related to the subject of this book. This site is updated regularly. Please use this link to access the list:

www.rosenlinks.com/taw/teag

# FOR FURTHER READING

Chisholm, Jane. *Usborne Encyclopedia of Ancient Greece*. London, England: Usborne Publishers, 2000.

Crosher, Judith. *Technology in the Time of Ancient Greece*. San Diego, CA: Raintree/Steck-Vaughn, 1998.

Ganeri, Anita. *Focus on Ancient Greeks*. New York, NY: Gloucester Press, 1993.

Jovinelly, Joann, and Jason Netelkos. *The Crafts and Cultures of the Ancient Greeks*. New York, NY: Rosen Publishing, 2002.

Kerr, Daisy, and Mark Bergin. *Ancient Greeks*. New York, NY: Franklin Watts, 1997.

MacDonald, Fiona, and Mark Bergin. *A Greek Temple*. New York, NY: Peter Bedrick Books, 1992.

Nardo, Don. *The Ancient Greeks* (Lost Civilizations). San Diego, CA: Greenhaven Press, 2000.

Pearson, Anne. *Eyewitness: Ancient Greece*. New York, NY: DK Publishing, 2000.

Woods, Michael, and Mary B. Woods. *Ancient Machines: From Wedges to Waterwheels* (Ancient Technology). Minneapolis, MN: Runestone Press, 2000.

Woods, Michael, and Mary B. Woods. *Ancient Warfare: From Clubs to Catapults* (Ancient Technology). Minneapolis, MN: Runestone Press, 2000.

# BIBLIOGRAPHY

Daniels, Patricia S., and Stephen G. Hyslop. *Almanac of World History*. Washington, DC: National Geographic Society, 2003.

Davis, Kevin A. *Look What Came from Greece*. New York, NY: Franklin Watts, 1999.

Durando, Furio. *Ancient Greece: The Dawn of the Western World*. New York, NY: Barnes and Noble Books, 2004.

Ganeri, Anita. *Focus on Ancient Greeks*. New York, NY: Gloucester Press, 1993.

Jovinelly, Joann, and Jason Netelkos. *The Crafts and Cultures of the Ancient Greeks*. New York, NY: Rosen Publishing, 2002.

MacDonald, Fiona, and Mark Bergin. *A Greek Temple*. New York, NY: Peter Bedrick Books, 1992.

Pearson, Anne. *Ancient Greece Eyewitness Books*. New York, NY: Dorling Kindersley, 1992.

Stuart, Gene S. "Greece and Rome." *Builders of the Ancient World Marvels of Engineering*. Washington, DC: National Geographic Society, 1986.

# INDEX

## A

Aeschylus, 20
Agamemnon, 32
agricultural methods, benefits of, 12
Alexander the Great, 8, 38
Archimedes, 11, 12, 36
Archimedes screw, 11–12
architecture, 7, 23–31
   amphitheaters, 31
   columns styles, 27
   houses, 25–26
   stadiums, 31
   temples, 26–29
Aristotle, 9, 38
astrolabe, 14

## B

botany, 9
Bronze Age, 5, 23

## C

Callicrates, 29
Classical Age, 5, 6, 7
clepsydra, 7
coins, 15
construction, 24–25
Corinth, 15–16
crops, 11
Ctesibius, 7

## D

Daedalus, 8
Darius, 34
Dark Age, 5, 6

## E

Erasistratus, 41
Eupalinos, 29
Eupalinos tunnel, 29
Euripides, 20

## H

Helen of Troy, 32
Hellenistic Age, 5, 8, 22
Herodotus, 21
Herophilus, 41
Hippocrates, 40–41
Homer, 20, 40

## I

Icarus, 8
Ictinus, 29
Iliad, The, 20, 32, 40

## L

Lion Gate, 24

## M

Menelaus, 32
Minoans, 5, 6, 17, 19, 23, 24
Minos, 5, 8
Mycenaeans, 5, 6, 18, 19, 32

## O

Odyssey, The, 20, 32

## P

palace at Knossos, 23–24
Paris of Troy, 32

Parthenon, 23, 27, 29–31
Peloponnesian War, 35
Persian Wars, 34–35
Phidias, 29, 30
Philip II, 38
plays, 20–21, 31
pottery, 12–13, 14

**R**

Roman Empire, 8

**S**

Sanctuary of Apollo, 23
ships, 14, 15–16
Sophocles, 20
statue of Athena, 29
statue of Zeus, 30–31

**T**

Temple of Asclepius, 39
Temple of Ceres, 23
Temple of Hera, 23
Theodorus, 24–25
Theophrastus, 9
trade, 5, 14, 15, 16, 18, 19
Trojan War, 20, 32

**W**

warfare
catapult, 36, 38
phalanx, 33
triremes, 35–37
writing, 17–22

**X**

Xerxes, 34

## About the Author

Charles W. Maynard is a writer who lives in Jonesborough, Tennessee. He has a great interest in ancient Greece and Rome, born from his study of Latin, Greek, and Hebrew. He is a graduate of Emory & Henry College and Emory University, and he continues to be fascinated with the history and myths of the ancient world.

## Photo Credits

Cover Erich Lessing/Art Resource, NY; p. 4 Vanni/Art Resource, NY; p. 6 Courtesy of the University of Texas Libraries, The University of Texas at Austin; p. 7 The Art Archive/Agora Museum Athens/Dagli Orti; pp. 10, 20–21 Bildarchiv Preussischer Kulturbesitz/Art Resource, NY; p. 12 The Art Archive/Musée du Louvre, Paris/Dagli Orti; p.13 © SSPL/The Image Works; p. 14 Erich Lessing/Art Resource, NY; p. 15 Snark/Art Resource, NY; p. 18 (top) The Art Archive/Heraklion Museum/Dagli Orti; p. 18 (bottom) The Art Archive/Archaeological Museum Chora Greece/Dagli Orti; p. 20 British Library; p. 24 © Third Eye Images/ Corbis; p. 25 Réunion des Musées Nationaux/Art Resource, NY; p. 26 akg-images/John Hios; p. 27 © ANA/The Image Works; pp. 28, 34–35 akg-images/Peter Connolly; p. 30 © Yann Arthus-Bertrand/Corbis; p. 33 © Gianni Dagli Orti/Corbis; p. 36 Galleria degli Uffizi/Bridgeman Art Library; p. 37 The Art Archive/Acropolis Museum Athens/Dagli Orti; p. 40 The Art Archive/Archaeological Museum Piraeus/Dagli Orti.

**Editor:** Kathy Kuhtz Campbell
**Designer:** Evelyn Horovicz
**Photo Researcher:** Amy Feinberg